MAR ▬▬▬

BANNED ~~BOOKS~~

The Controversy Over What Students Read

Meryl Loonin

ReferencePoint
Press®

San Diego, CA

About the Author

This is Meryl Loonin's seventh book for young adult readers. She has worked in documentary film and TV and cofounded an organization to support library programming for teens. She lives in historic Lexington, Massachusetts.

Picture Credits:
Cover: Pawel_B/iStock

6: ZUMA Press, Inc./Alamy Stock Photo
11: Maury Aaseng
14: wavebreakmedia/Shutterstock
16: Ben Molyneux/Alamy Stock Photo
20: Associated Press
23: SuperStock/Alamy Stock Photo
25: Everett Collection Inc/Alamy Stock Photo

29: Ian Macpherson London/Alamy Stock Photo
32: Art Directors & TRIP/Alamy Stock Photo
35: OntheRun photo/Alamy Stock Photo
39: sjbooks/Alamy Stock Photo
41: ton koene/Alamy Stock Photo
45: WENN Rights Ltd/Alamy Stock Photo
49: Stephen Saks Photography/Alamy Stock Photo
51: CBW/Alamy Stock Photo
55: Associated Press

LIBRARY OF CONGRESS CATALOGING-IN-PUBLICATION DATA

Names: Loonin Meryl, author.
Title: Banned Books: The Controversy Over What Students Read/ by Meryl Loonin.
Description: San Diego : ReferencePoint Press, 2023. | Includes
  bibliographical references and index.
Identifiers: LCCN: 2022045182
(print)| 9781678204747 (library binding) |
  ISBN 9781678204778 (ebook)
Subjects: LCSH: book banning--United States--Juvenile
  literature. | literature--Moral and ethical aspects--United
  States--Juvenile literature.

CONTENTS

A New Wave of Book Banning

On October 25, 2021, Texas state legislator Matt Krause emailed a letter to state and local school officials that sparked a rise in book banning across the nation. In the letter, Krause announced his inquiry into books and other content in Texas schools. Attached to his email was a sixteen-page spreadsheet listing 850 books, many of them focused on stories and issues of race, gender identity, and sexuality. To aid in his investigation, Krause requested that school officials report back on how many copies of the 850 books they discovered in classrooms and libraries, along with any other books that might cause students to "feel discomfort, guilt, anguish, or any other form of psychological distress because of their race or sex."[1]

Krause's political rivals dismissed his letter as a "politically motivated stunt,"[2] but many teachers and librarians were alarmed by it. "What will Representative Krause propose next?" asked Ovidia Molina, president of the Texas State Teachers Association. "Burning books he and a handful of parents find objectionable?"[3]

School officials were split over how to respond. School district administrators in Dallas and Austin ignored the letter. But in Granbury, a city of about ten thousand near the Dallas–Fort Worth metro area, the school district pulled 130 books from library shelves, pending investigation. And in San Antonio, a South Texas city of 1.5 million, the school district pulled 432 books off library shelves.

The Perfect Storm for a Culture War

Before Krause sent his letter, parents in several Texas school districts—and elsewhere in the country—had sought to ban books that addressed race and LGBTQ issues. His letter ramped up these book-banning efforts. By 2022 there were more books banned from school libraries in Texas than any other state. After the list of books went viral online, parents and politicians across the nation demanded the removal of many of its titles. Krause's list fanned the flames of a growing national culture war.

While cultural conflict over race and gender issues in America had been brewing for years, many observers trace the roots of the latest culture war to the summer of 2020, when social and political forces created the perfect storm for it. The country was reeling under the strain and uncertainty of the deadly COVID-19 pandemic; its politics

> "What will Representative [Matt] Krause propose next? Burning books he and a handful of parents find objectionable?"[3]
>
> —Ovidia Molina, president of the Texas State Teachers Association

were hyperpolarized and combative. Starting in late May, Black Lives Matter protests erupted in cities across the country in response to the brutal police killing of an unarmed Black man named George Floyd in Minneapolis. Floyd was one in a long line of Black people killed by excessive police violence, and his death was a wake-up call. Many US institutions—businesses, nonprofits, government agencies, and schools—began to confront the racism in their organizations. They hosted antiracism trainings, announced diversity measures, and launched ad campaigns to show their support for racial equality or committed to achieving it. Cultural commentators noted that this nationwide reckoning with racism in American society echoed louder, and longer, than at any time in recent history.

The backlash, spurred on by racially charged comments from then-president Donald Trump and right-wing media pundits, was loud and resounding, too. It soon grew to include outrage over young people's changing attitudes about gender identity and sexual orientation. By late 2020 these issues were driving much of

5

In 2021 Texas state lawmaker Matt Krause (pictured) announced an investigation into 850 books that he says could make students feel discomfort because of their race or sex. His letter to state officials and the list that accompanied it sparked a rise in book bans across the nation.

right-wing media coverage and political campaigning. That same year new conservative parent groups, including Moms for Liberty and No Left Turn in Education (NLTE), got their start and expanded to include local chapters across the nation. Public schools became culture war battlegrounds. Parents linked to these groups or inspired by them flooded into school board meetings to demand that books on race and LGBTQ issues be removed from their children's libraries and classrooms.

Protecting Young People

In the name of protecting young people, parents have often sought to ban books from schools and libraries. In the 1980s and again in the early 2000s, they targeted books that contained profanity, sex, drug use, witchcraft, or characters that disrespected authority.

Parents described these books as undermining their family values and teachings or exposing their children to corrupting influences.

In the latest wave of book banning, the titles that have come under the fiercest attack explore LGBTQ and racial justice issues or are written by people of color and LGBTQ authors. The adults who object to these books claim that they promote immoral lifestyles and cause their own children to feel uncomfortable or ashamed solely because they are White and heterosexual.

The Power of Suppressing Books

The latest wave of book banning is unprecedented in its scope. According to the American Library Association (ALA), there were more attempts to ban books in 2021 than at any time since the group began tracking three decades earlier. These efforts are not limited to books or libraries. Many states have also passed extreme new censorship laws that restrict what teachers and students can read and discuss in the classroom. Free speech defenders say the laws are a threat to intellectual freedom—and to democracy itself.

Leaders of the world's most brutal, authoritarian regimes have long understood the power of suppressing books and ideas. In 1933 the Nazis staged massive public book burnings across Germany. Helen Keller, the deaf and blind American disability activist and socialist, was one of the authors whose works were targeted. When she learned that pro-Nazi student groups were rounding up books to be

> "History has taught you nothing if you think you can kill ideas. You can burn my books and the books of the best minds in Europe, but the ideas in them have seeped through a million channels and will continue to quicken other minds."[4]
>
> —Helen Keller, disability rights activist

burned, she wrote them an open letter. "History has taught you nothing if you think you can kill ideas," she wrote. "You can burn my books and the books of the best minds in Europe, but the ideas in them have seeped through a million channels and will continue to quicken other minds."[4]

CHAPTER ONE

Book Bans, Culture Wars, and the Freedom to Read

Every fall, librarians, booksellers, publishers, free speech advocates, and avid readers across the country prepare for Banned Books Week, an annual celebration of the freedom to read. There are catchy slogans, "I read banned books" posters and T-shirts, and library displays of the books that the ALA identifies as the most challenged titles of the year. The books are wrapped in caution tape—or their covers are concealed—to evoke the spirit of rebel readers around the world who have risked imprisonment or even death to read and discuss literature while living under repressive regimes. Many public libraries and bookstores host Banned Books Week events, including Stand for the Banned Read-Outs, which are dramatic readings of excerpts from banned books, and Dear Banned Author letter-writing campaigns, which encourage readers to write, tweet, or email a favorite author whose books have been banned. The events may seem lighthearted, but the purpose behind them is serious: to raise awareness of the dangers of censorship and protect freedoms that are at the heart of American democracy—to access information and express ideas.

Banned Books Week got its start in 1982, at a time when the country was embroiled in another culture war. Republican president Ronald Reagan was serving in the White House—and the Moral Majority, a right-wing evangelical Christian group, exerted growing influence over the nation's politics and culture. The ALA and other free speech groups were alarmed by a sharp rise in book-banning attempts in US schools, public libraries, and bookstores. They launched Banned Books Week to call attention to the growing censorship threat. Decades later, with book banning once again on the rise, librarians say Banned Books Week has become more vital than ever before.

> "It's painful to me because what I know is that when these books are banned, there are going to be thousands and thousands of young people who will not get these books."[5]
>
> —Jason Reynolds, children's and YA author

Over the years, works by many critically acclaimed authors have appeared on the ALA's annual list of the most challenged books. Award-winning author Jason Reynolds writes popular hip hop–infused, young adult (YA) books with narratives that center on Black teen boys. When his books are challenged and banned, he worries about the young readers who lose access to stories with diverse characters and perspectives. "It's painful to me because what I know is that when these books are banned, there are going to be thousands and thousands of young people who will not get these books,"[5] he says.

Bans, Challenges, and Soft Censorship

The ALA first began tracking instances of book banning in 1990. The organization counts both the number of times a book is banned outright and removed from library shelves and when it is challenged—meaning someone attempts to ban it. Most school and public libraries have formal procedures in place to handle book challenges. The person or group seeking a book's removal submit a form explaining the objections. This triggers a formal review process. Usually, a committee made up of librarians, teachers, school administrators, and community members read the book and consider the motivations for the challenge before making a final decision.

In 2021 the ALA reported more books being challenged than at any time since it began tracking: 729 separate efforts to censor almost 1,600 different books. In a typical year there are 300 to 400 challenges, and most are lodged against a single title. The bulk of these challenges occur in public schools. PEN America, an advocacy group that defends freedom of speech and expression, conducted its own in-depth survey of book banning in US public schools over nine months in 2021 and 2022. The group reported 1,586 separate book bans, including "removals of books from school libraries, prohibitions from reading them in classrooms, or both, as well as books banned from circulation."[6] These were carried out in eighty-six different school districts in twenty-six different states.

But these numbers are just the tip of the iceberg, because most book challenges and bans—as many as 90 percent, according to the ALA—go unreported or take place out of the public eye. Books for young people are far more likely to fall prey to soft censorship. "Soft censorship is that dirty little secret,"[7] says *School Library Journal* book reviewer Kiera Parrott. It happens when a book is quietly removed from school library shelves and disappears. A book may also be flagged to restrict access, or schools may require a parent's permission before students can borrow it. Sometimes books are hidden in a locked cabinet or behind the reference desk, so students are forced to ask the librarian to retrieve them. The most widespread type of soft censorship occurs after national headline-grabbing book bans. These may cause a school administrator to quietly remove a book, librarians to think twice before adding it to their collections, or teachers to omit it from the curriculum, because they fear stirring up controversy in their own communities.

What Makes the New Wave of Book Banning Different?

Many young people today have access to instant information online. By their late teens, many have been exposed to misinformation, hate speech, sexual content, violence, and profanity via their smartphones, TV, social media, and video games. Yet conservative parent groups and politicians are focused on removing books from schools and libraries. In their view, books in schools pose a

The Ten Most Challenged Books of 2021

Every year the American Library Association (ALA) tracks challenges to books and other materials in libraries, schools, and universities. In 2021 the ALA's Office for Intellectual Freedom tracked 729 such challenges involving 1,597 books. The ten most challenged books, and the reasons for the challenges, appear below. For all ten, the challenges led to bans.

Challenged and Banned: The Top Ten

	Book and Author	Reasons
1	*Gender Queer* by Maia Kobabe	LGBTQ content, considered to have sexually explicit images
2	*Lawn Boy* by Jonathan Evison	LGBTQ content, considered to be sexually explicit
3	*All Boys Aren't Blue* by George M. Johnson	LGBTQ content, profanity, considered to be sexually explicit
4	*Out of Darkness* by Ashley Hope Perez	Depictions of abuse, considered to be sexually explicit
5	*The Hate U Give* by Angie Thomas	Profanity, violence, thought to promote an anti-police message and indoctrination of a social agenda
6	*The Absolutely True Diary of a Part-Time Indian* by Sherman Alexie	Profanity, sexual references, use of a derogatory term
7	*Me and Earl and the Dying Girl* by Jesse Andrews	Considered to be sexually explicit and degrading to women
8	*The Bluest Eye* by Toni Morrison	Depicts child sexual abuse, considered to be sexually explicit
9	*This Book is Gay* by Juno Dawson	Sexual education, LGBTQ content
10	*Beyond Magenta* by Susan Kuklin	LGBTQ content, considered to be sexually explicit

Source: "Top 10 Most Challenged Books Lists," American Library Association. www.ala.org/advocacy/bbooks/frequentlychallengedbooks/top10.

particular threat to young people. NLTE founder Elana Fishbein declares that her group "is standing up against activist educators who are placing obscene, pornographic, racist, and hateful material in the hands of children."[8]

Free speech advocates say that book banning is an attack not only on books but also on the democratic institutions—public schools and libraries—where free access to ideas and information is a core value. And although it is books that are being challenged, the culture war itself is waged on newer media, as parents share book titles and strategies on social media platforms and among chapters of national conservative parent groups like NLTE. The outrage spreads faster and further than anyone living through the book-banning surge of the 1980s could have imagined.

The new wave of book banning is a departure from the past in other ways, too. In earlier book bans, demands that titles be removed from school libraries usually started with concerned parents in the local community. In contrast, during the nine months covered by the PEN America survey, more than 40 percent of book bans were linked to directives from state officials or elected lawmakers. The survey's authors say this is a disturbing trend: schools often respond to these directives by ignoring their own review procedures and overruling the professional judgment of teachers and librarians.

Free speech advocates are also deeply concerned about a spate of restrictive censorship laws that make book banning easier and limit what teachers can discuss about race and LGBTQ issues in the classroom. "There's a meaningful difference," writes *Atlantic* journalist Emma Sarappo, a critic of the new laws, "between parents communicating concern directly to schools and the government stepping in with sweeping intimidation tactics."[9]

> "There's a meaningful difference between parents communicating concern directly to schools and the government stepping in with sweeping intimidation tactics."[9]
>
> —Emma Sarappo, *Atlantic* magazine journalist

Upholding Students' Freedom to Read

When students at a New York high school learned that the school board had secretly removed eleven books from their school library, they sued the school district. Their case, *Board of Education, Island Trees Union Free School District v. Pico*, eventually reached the Supreme Court, which ruled in the students' favor in 1982.

The lawsuit, filed by the American Civil Liberties Union on behalf of Steven Pico and five other students, contended that the removal of the books violated the students' First Amendment rights. The books had all appeared on a target list compiled by a conservative parent group. Among them were *Slaughterhouse-Five*, an anti-war novel by author Kurt Vonnegut; an anthology of short stories by Black writers edited by Harlem Renaissance writer and poet Langston Hughes; and *Go Ask Alice*, a YA novel billed as the real diary of a teenage girl in which she described her harrowing downward spiral into drug addiction.

The 1982 central ruling in *Pico* still holds today. It says, "Local school boards may not remove books from school libraries simply because they dislike the ideas contained in those books and seek by their removal to 'prescribe what shall be orthodox in politics, nationalism, religion, or other matters of opinion.'"

Board of Education, Island Trees Union Free School District No. 26 v. Pico, 457 US 854, 1982.

Under Fire: Diverse Young Adult Books

In another striking shift from the past, the books that have been most fiercely targeted in recent years are YA titles that amplify once marginalized voices and explore racially diverse and LGBTQ issues and perspectives. In 2020, the year of George Floyd's killing by police and of the Black Lives Matter protests, the ALA reported that many of the most challenged books of the year dealt with racism and Black American history. In 2021 the list was made up largely of books dealing with LGBTQ issues.

Many of these books would not have existed just a decade ago. In recent years the publishing industry has grappled with its own racial and diversity reckoning. Change has been slow, but today young people have access to more diverse titles than ever before. Among the most challenged books of 2020 and 2021 are *All Boys Aren't Blue* by George M. Johnson, a series of personal

A student looks for a book in her school library. More books were challenged in 2021 than at any time since tracking began—and most of those challenges occurred in public schools.

essays, in which the author describes growing up queer and Black; *The Hate U Give* by Angie Thomas, a novel about a Black teen girl who finds her voice after witnessing a friend's killing at the hands of police; and *Out of Darkness* by Ashley Hope Pérez, a historical novel set in 1930s Texas that centers on a forbidden interracial teen romance, child sexual abuse, and a deadly school gas explosion. These books do not shy away from frank portrayals of sex, violence, mental health struggles, and other edgy topics. But free speech advocates say it is no coincidence that they feature racially diverse and LGBTQ characters and experiences and address many of the same issues that fuel the larger culture war.

Canceling Culturally and Racially Insensitive Books

Conservative parents and politicians are behind the latest wave of book banning. Yet liberal activists, cultural critics, and others on the left have also challenged books. These challenges target books that they perceive as culturally or racially insensitive, or that

14

are written by authors whose behavior or opinions are viewed by many progressives as offensive. When these activists launch social media hashtag campaigns that exert pressure to boycott or publicly shame a performer, creator, author, or other public figure, they are often accused of taking part in cancel culture.

Sometimes the pressure on authors and publishers is so intense, they cancel their own books before they arrive on bookstore and library shelves. In 2016 a new children's picture book that portrayed George Washington's slave Hercules and his young daughter happily baking a birthday cake for the first president was blasted by left-leaning groups for sugarcoating slavery. After a fierce social media backlash, the publisher, Scholastic, pulled

Young Adult Authors Speak Out

While some authors are defiant when their books are banned, others describe it as a painful experience. In the latest wave of book banning, YA titles by Angie Thomas and Ashley Hope Pérez have been frequently attacked. In *The Hate U Give*, a Black teen girl struggles to come to terms with her grief and anger after witnessing a police officer kill her childhood friend. Critics say its message is anti-police. Thomas counters that it is "anti-police brutality." When she first learned that her book had been banned, she says, "I was just shellshocked, and then I felt hurt. . . . More so than attacking me, it felt like they were attacking the kids from my neighborhood, and other kids like them."

Pérez's *Out of Darkness* is set in 1930s East Texas, where she grew up, and centers on a forbidden romance between a Mexican American teen girl and a Black teen boy. It has been challenged for explicit content, including a rape scene. "It's a damaging myth that removing a story about painful aspects of human experience will in any way protect young people," she says. "This is like arguing that a school-wide moratorium on discussions of bullying will eliminate the problem. Silence is the real threat."

Quoted in Leonard S. Marcus, ed., *You Can't Say That! Writers for Young People Talk About Censorship, Free Expression, and the Stories They Have to Tell*. Somerville, MA: Candlewick, 2021, p. 199.

Ashley Hope Pérez, "I Wrote *Out of Darkness* for My High School Students, Now High Schools Are Removing It," *Dallas (TX) Morning News*, February 11, 2022. www.dallasnews.com.

it from circulation. "Stories matter," wrote YA author Daniel José Older, in defense of the cancellation campaign, "and the stakes are higher in children's literature."[10]

Yet free speech groups called the book's removal troubling. They predicted that pulling it from circulation would cause authors and illustrators to hesitate before taking on racially sensitive topics again. "The power of online indignation to remove books from circulation should worry anyone who believes in free speech,"[11] writes PEN America executive director Suzanne Nossel.

Protecting the Right to Read

Librarians and teachers regularly make decisions about what to include, exclude, or weed out from classroom and library shelves to update their collections, and they sometimes cull racially or culturally insensitive books. The ALA draws a sharp distinction between this process and demands by parents and politicians to remove books.

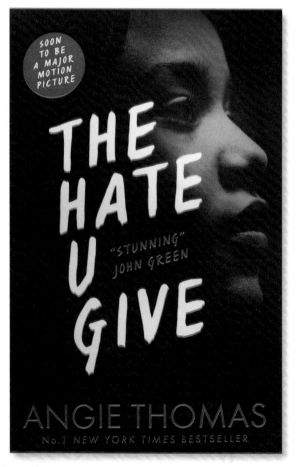

Selecting books based on professional guidelines is *not* the same thing as censorship. Most librarians strive to create collections that appeal to the widest diversity of students—or library patrons—in their communities. They consult reliable sources and book award lists and consider what aligns with school curricula. They check in with colleagues, follow blogs,

Young adult books that amplify once-marginalized voices have been targeted in recent years. Among the most challenged books of 2020 and 2021 is The Hate U Give, *a novel about a Black teen who finds her voice after witnessing a friend's killing by police.*

and use online forums. Age appropriate-
ness is also a factor. Librarians may also
reject or weed out books that are mis-
leading, are factually inaccurate, or that
contain racist, anti-LGBTQ, anti-Semitic,
or other hateful content.

Librarians are trained to resist book banning and censorship.
"Our obligation," writes public librarian Lucy Bellamy, "is to defend
and protect children's freedom to read, and to make sure they
have access to rich and extensive collections."[12]

The Courts Weigh In

In 1982, the same year as the ALA's first-ever Banned Books
Week, the Supreme Court issued a decision in a landmark school
library book-banning case. It is known as *Board of Education, Island Trees Union Free School District v. Pico*. The *Pico* case centered on a high school in Long Island, New York, where school
board members secretly removed eleven books (two were later
returned) from the library. According to court records, the board
members claimed the books were "anti-American, anti-Christian,
anti-Semitic, and just plain filthy."[13] In a narrow 5–4 decision, the
court ruled that schools may not restrict students' access to
books simply because they disagree with the ideas the books
contain. Yet *Pico* ended in a fractured decision. The five justices
in the majority did not agree on the legal basis for the ruling. This
left the door open for banning books on other grounds. As stat-
ed in the court's decision, books might be removed if they are
deemed "pervasively vulgar" or "educationally unsuitable."[14] With
book bans once again surging—and opponents filing lawsuits to
stop them—legal scholars say the meanings of these hard-to-
pin-down terms are about to be tested.

CHAPTER TWO

Banned and Challenged: Books That Address Race

The political ad dropped in the final days of a hotly contested 2021 race for Virginia governor. Within the first twenty-four hours of its release, it had been viewed more than 1 million times. It was reported to have spurred Republican voters to go to the polls and secure victory for their candidate, wealthy businessman Glenn Youngkin. In a warmly lit room with flames flickering in the fireplace and family photos on the mantle, Fairfax County mother Laura Murphy speaks to the camera. "As a parent, it's tough to catch everything," she says, "but when my son showed me his reading assignment, my heart sunk. It was some of the most explicit material that you can imagine."[15]

In the ad, Murphy blamed Youngkin's Democratic opponent, former governor Terry McAuliffe, for twice vetoing a bill that would have forced public school teachers to notify parents when they assigned sexually explicit reading material. Although the ad never mentioned the assignment that had upset Murphy, Youngkin's political opponents filled in the blanks. It was the Pulitzer Prize–winning novel *Beloved* by author Toni Morrison. Ten years earlier, Murphy's son was enrolled in a senior year Advanced Placement English class when he told his mother that *Beloved* was giving him night terrors. In 2013 Laura Murphy had tried—and failed—to persuade the Fairfax County school board to remove the novel from her son's curriculum.

Most people who read *Beloved* agree that it is a difficult, haunting book. It grapples with the brutality of slavery—and the trauma suffered by enslaved women who were frequently raped and exploited by White slaveowners. Morrison, a preeminent US literary figure and Nobel laureate, based the story on actual historical events. For years,

Beloved had been assigned in Fairfax County's college-level Advanced Placement English class, but the political atmosphere had changed. A little over a year had elapsed since the police killing of George Floyd, and a culture war was raging. Youngkin's campaign slogan "Parents Matter" and his promise to ban antiracist curricula in public schools resonated with many of the state's voters.

Uproar over Critical Race Theory

Weeks after Youngkin was sworn into office as Virginia's new governor, the state legislature sent him the parental notification bill for his signature. The new law requires teachers to seek parents' approval before assigning books deemed to be sexually explicit. On his first day in office, Youngkin also kept another popular campaign promise. He signed an executive order prohibiting the teaching of critical race theory in Virginia's public schools.

Before the summer of 2020, most people had never heard of critical race theory, but it had since become the new buzzword on right-wing media. According to the media tracking service Critical Mention, there were 132 references to critical race theory on the Fox News Channel in 2020, and 1,860 in the first six months of 2021. The frenzy of media coverage gave some people the impression that critical race theory posed an imminent danger. In reality, it is a nearly forty-year-old academic framework, taught mainly on college campuses and in law schools, that examines how historical patterns of racism are systemic—or embedded in America's institutions, laws, and policies. While most people think

19

On his first day in office, Governor Glenn Youngkin of Virginia signs an executive order prohibiting the teaching of critical race theory in Virginia's public schools.

of racism as a product of individual biases and prejudices, proponents of critical race theory argue that even people who do not intend to behave in racist ways often make choices that drive racial inequality because racism is part of systems of employment, education, health care, housing, and other areas of life.

Yet critical race theory's founders say it has been distorted beyond recognition. It is portrayed by right-wing media as a divisive, fringe ideology that pits people of different races against each other and faults all White people for being inherently racist. Critical race theory has become a catchall for almost any ideas, practices, books, and materials that examine America's racial history and attempt to shed light on the racial inequities that persist today.

Suppressing America's Troubled Racial History

In a single year critical race theory morphed from an obscure academic framework into a conservative rallying cry. During that same time, it also migrated from right-wing TV talk shows to the halls of state government. By June 2022 lawmakers in forty-two states had introduced bills or other measures to limit teaching about racism and sexism in the classroom. Many stalled or failed to pass, but legislators in at least seventeen states passed laws to ban the teaching of critical race theory and other so-called divisive concepts in K–12 public schools. In other states, anti–critical race theory measures were imposed by departments of education or local school boards. While there is no evidence that critical race theory is taught in any K–12 public schools, defenders of the divisive concepts laws say that its core ideas are.

The laws vary by state, but most are adapted from an executive order called Combating Race and Sex Stereotyping, signed by former president Donald Trump in September 2020. Although the order was overturned by his successor, Joe Biden, much of its language survives in the new state laws. These laws prohibit teachers from discussing topics in the classroom that promote racist or sexist stereotyping, undermine American values, or cause some students to feel discomfort or other distress.

Over the years, US courts have ruled that school and government officials may exercise control over public school curricula, deciding which topics, concepts, or books to cover, without trampling on the rights of K–12 students or educators. School officials and politicians who support the divisive concepts laws say this is exactly what they are doing. "We can and should teach this history without labeling a young child as an oppressor or requiring he or she feel guilt or shame based on their race or sex,"[16] argues Oklahoma governor J. Kevin Stitt.

Free speech groups counter that the divisive concepts laws threaten students' academic freedom—and likely violate the US Constitution's First Amendment prohibition on government laws abridging Americans' freedom of speech. In a 2021 report, PEN America dubbed the laws educational gag orders. Says Jonathan Friedman, PEN America's director of free expression and education, the laws "muzzle entire subject areas, scare teachers from engaging in important discussions, and deprive students of opportunities to ask questions, learn, and grow."[17]

> "[Educational gag orders] muzzle entire subject areas, scare teachers from engaging in important discussions, and deprive students of opportunities to ask questions, learn, and grow."[17]
>
> —Jonathan Friedman, PEN America's director of free expression and education

The 1619 Project

The 1619 Project is named for the year that the first ship carrying enslaved Africans arrived at American shores. It was released as a special issue of the *New York Times Magazine* in 2019 and later turned into articles, books, and school curricula. Led by journalist Hannah Nikole-Jones, with input from prominent Black writers, the introduction to the 1619 Project explains that "it aims to reframe US history by placing the consequences of slavery and the contributions of black Americans at the very center of our national narrative."

Many historians and educators have praised the Pulitzer Prize–winning project for shedding light on slavery and its legacy in American life. Politicians on the right have denounced it as dangerous propaganda. In September 2020 President Donald Trump called it "ideological poison" that, if not removed, will "destroy our country." He convened a 1776 Commission and ordered federal agencies to promote "a patriotic education" that would instill pride in America.

Following Trump's lead, states dominated by conservative lawmakers have prohibited teaching the 1619 Project in public schools. Free speech groups warn that it is undemocratic to single out a work of scholarship that politicians disagree with and censor it by law.

"The 1619 Project," *New York Times Magazine*, August 14, 2019. https://nytimes.com.

Quoted in Judy Woodruff, "What Trump Is Saying About 1619 Project, Teaching U.S. History," *PBS NewsHour*, September 17, 2020. www.pbs.org.

The laws are so broadly worded that teachers report avoiding any discussion of racial justice issues out of fear of upsetting parents or students or losing their jobs. PEN America warns that these laws whitewash history, erase the experiences of students of color, and prevent all students from reckoning honestly with America's past.

The Parents' Rights Movement

Many of the divisive concepts laws also include provisions that make it easier for parents to challenge books, monitor classroom curricula, and sue schools that do not comply. This is part of a parents' rights agenda, supported by groups like NLTE and Moms for Liberty. "We're disrupting the balance of power in public education," says Moms for Liberty cofounder Tina Descovich. "Our number one goal is to help parents speak up for their parental rights."[18]

Free speech advocates warn that this push for parents' rights is often a pretext for trying to block educators from introducing diverse books and curricula and affirming the rights of non-White, LGBTQ, and other marginalized groups. Education policy scholar Leslie Fenwick explains that parents' rights movements have a troubling history in America. After the Supreme Court's landmark *Brown v. Board of Education* decision in 1954, which prohibited segregation in public schools, educators tried to add Black Americans' achievements to school history textbooks. "White parents burned books, physically threatened White teachers who tried to teach the more inclusive curriculum and pressured school boards not to adopt books and curriculum that featured anything Black,"[19] Fenwick says.

Over the decades, US courts have granted parents broad authority to decide how to educate their own kids. But when they try to ban books and curricula for an entire school community, they are on shakier legal ground. At that point, free speech groups argue, they are infringing on the academic freedom of other people's children.

Free speech groups warn that the divisive concepts laws passed in various states threaten students' academic freedom. They also argue that these laws violate the First Amendment prohibition on government laws abridging freedom of speech.

CONGRESS SHALL MAKE NO LAW *respecting an establishment of religion, or prohibiting the free exercise thereof; or abridging the freedom of speech, or of the press; or the right of the people peaceably to assemble, and to petition the Government for a redress of grievances.*

❧ THE FIRST AMENDMENT TO THE U.S. CONSTITUTION
15 DECEMBER 1791

Banning Diverse Children's Books

Amid the panic over critical race theory, there has been a dramatic rise in efforts to challenge and ban children's books by Black and Brown authors. Spurred on by the passage of the divisive concepts laws in many states, conservative parent groups have demanded that schools remove children's books that they believe sow racial division. In July 2021 a Tennessee chapter of the group Moms for Liberty filed a complaint against second-grade picture book biographies of civil rights heroes Martin Luther King Jr. and Ruby Bridges. At age six, Bridges became the first Black child to integrate an all-white school in the South. In 1960 Bridges had to be escorted by federal marshals through a jeering white mob that threatened to lynch and poison her. When children read her book she says, "I truly want them to understand. The racism just does not make any sense."[20] The Moms for Liberty group charged that the King and Bridges books had "a heavily biased agenda, one that makes children hate their country, each other, and/or themselves."[21]

Racist Content in Decades-Old Children's Books

In March 2021 Dr. Seuss Enterprises—the company run by the family of Theodor Seuss Geisel (aka Dr. Seuss)—caused a backlash on social media with its announcement that it would stop printing six of the beloved author's lesser-known titles. The books, including *If I Ran the Zoo*, *McElligot's Pool*, and *On Beyond Zebra*, contain offensive racist caricatures of Black, Asian, and Arab people.

Dr. Seuss's whimsical rhymes and illustrations have long been a staple of childhood. Conservative pundits and politicians fumed on social media that left-wing cancel culture had come for a giant of children's literature. Yet many psychological studies have shown that children begin to internalize racial bias early, between the ages of two and four; by age ten, many of these biases are fixed. Besides titles by Dr. Seuss, progressive educators and parents have begun to reexamine other old picture book favorites. "We must evaluate books for children by today's values, not on our own nostalgia," says children's literature professor Ann Neely. "Children need to see themselves, and others who may be different from them, in an accurate and positive way."

Quoted in Char Adams, "The Reckoning with Dr. Seuss' Racist Imagery Has Been Years in the Making," NBC News, March 3, 2021. www.nbcnews.com.

Some parent groups have tried to ban picture book biographies of civil rights heroes, including one about Ruby Bridges (pictured in 2022). At age six she became the first Black child to integrate an all-White school in Louisiana.

Parent groups have also pushed to ban fictional children's books with diverse characters and stories. In October 2021 four hundred parents in Southlake, a suburb of Dallas, Texas, signed a petition demanding that school officials cancel a virtual school visit with author Jerry Craft. The parents also demanded that school officials stop promoting Kraft's middle grade graphic novel, *New Kid*, and its sequel, *Class Act*. The Newbery Medal–awarded *New Kid* is a humorous account of a Black teen who navigates life—and racism—at an elite private middle school. "The books don't come out and say we want white children to feel like oppressors, but that is absolutely what they will do,"[22] said Bonnie Anderson, one of the parents behind the petition.

Mirrors, Windows, and Sliding Glass Doors

In 2021, as the culture war raged, the most challenged books in America were YA titles with racially diverse characters and stories.

Angie Thomas's *The Hate U Give*, which centers on the story of a Black teen killed by police, and Ibram X. Kendi's and Jason Reynold's *Stamped: Racism, Anti-racism, and You*, which describes the history of racist ideas in America and proposes antiracist ideas to replace them, were among the books frequently targeted.

The fact that many of these diverse titles exist at all represents a sea change in the publishing industry. For decades, children's and YA books were dominated by White authors, characters, and stories. In 1965 educator Nancy Larrick wrote an eye-opening article in *Saturday Review* magazine entitled "The All-White World of Children's Books." It was inspired by a five-year-old girl who asked Larrick why all the stories she read were about White children. By Larrick's estimate, only four-fifths of 1 percent of all US children's books being published at the time included contemporary Black characters.

In the years since, there has been slow progress. The Cooperative Children's Book Center estimated that 27 percent of all children's and YA books released by US publishing houses in 2019 included a non-White primary character. The 2019 data also showed that roughly 83 percent of children's and YA books were still written or illustrated by White authors or artists. Yet a majority of US public school students—29 million of the 49.4 million total—are either non-White or biracial.

Literature helps shape the worldviews of children and teens. Educators say they need books that provide mirrors, windows, and sliding glass doors—an idea coined by education scholar Rudine Sims Bishop. Books are sometimes windows, she explained, offering views of worlds that are different from readers' own. When those windows become sliding glass doors, readers can enter them in imagination. And if the light is just right, the windows turn into mirrors, reflecting and affirming readers' own lives. When diverse books are banned, educators say, it suggests that some narratives and stories have more value than others. Young people of color are less likely to see themselves reflected in their books—and White children and teens are less likely to develop empathy for others who do not share their racial identity.

CHAPTER THREE

Banned and Challenged: Books with LGBTQ Themes

In June 2022 the ALA Office for Intellectual Freedom became aware of a disturbing trend: the books in library LGBTQ Pride displays were disappearing. Nationwide, there were dozens of such incidents, and each one followed a similar pattern. Patrons arrived at the library, gathered up the books from the displays, and checked them all out at once, leaving the shelves empty. Within days librarians received letters that began this way: "To protect our children and the community, we have checked out the books in the pride display. We plan to keep these books checked out until the library agrees to remove the inappropriate content from the shelves."[23]

To many librarians, it was not surprising that these incidents of vigilante censorship were happening in June, which is recognized in many parts of the country and the world as LGBTQ Pride Month. June marks the anniversary of the historic Stonewall uprising of 1969. That year patrons of the Stonewall Inn—a popular gay bar in New York City—staged six days of protests and street demonstrations that are widely viewed as the birth of the modern LGBTQ rights movement. At the time, LGBTQ people were subject

> "To protect our children and the community, we have checked out the books in the pride display. We plan to keep these books checked out until the library agrees to remove the inappropriate content from the shelves."[23]
>
> —Letters sent to librarians

to discriminatory laws and persecution. They could be denied services, ousted from their jobs, harassed by police, or even arrested and jailed. Stonewall spurred more people to come out as gay to their families and communities and push for LGBTQ civil rights.

Many libraries celebrate Pride Month by decorating walls with rainbow banners, hosting Pride story times and author visits, and displaying books that reflect the lives and experiences of LGBTQ Americans. In recent years, June has also been a time when the ALA has seen a spike in book challenges, bans, and other complaints. Typically, these have been isolated incidents. In contrast, the reports flooding into the ALA Office for Intellectual Freedom in June 2022 suggested a coordinated, nationwide censorship campaign. The sponsor of this campaign was a conservative group called CatholicVote (with no actual affiliation to the Catholic Church).

The ALA issued a strong rebuke. "The language used by this organization is couched in terms of child protection," warned Deborah Caldwell-Stone, director of the Office for Intellectual Freedom, "but . . . this group is promoting an unethical and hateful censorship tactic."[24] Despite her defiant words, the campaign produced a chilling effect. On social media platforms and blogs, librarians shared with colleagues that they would hesitate before putting up a Pride display again.

A Backlash to Changing Social Norms

By the time of the crusade to dismantle library Pride displays, LGBTQ issues—and the banning of so-called rainbow books— were at the center of the country's growing culture war. For years, some conservative groups had fought against granting civil rights to LGBTQ Americans, but their views had not prevailed. The Supreme Court legalized same-sex marriage across the country in 2015, LGBTQ soldiers serve openly in the military, Pride parades attract hundreds of thousands of people each year, and polls showed in 2020 that a majority of Americans support LGBTQ rights.

Now right-wing politicians and parent groups have seized on a new issue: changing norms around gender identity. People who are

transgender (not identifying with the sex assigned to them at birth) and nonbinary (neither a man nor a woman, or not strictly one or the other) have become more visible in American popular culture. They appear on TV and social media, in movies, books, and even the Marvel Comics universe. But as acceptance of nonconforming gender identities has grown, so has the right-wing backlash. A 2022 Pew Research Center survey found that many older Americans were uncomfortable with the rapid pace of change around issues of gender identity and sexual orientation. Among Republican voters—and those who identified as evangelical Christians—the level of discomfort was far greater. The Pew Research Center survey also found a wide generational divide, with young adults "at the leading edge of change and acceptance."[25]

In the country's hyperpolarized climate, journalists report that Republican politicians are ratcheting up their anti-LGBTQ rhetoric to rally supporters. On the campaign trail, they aim some of their

The Controversy over a Penguin Story

The children's picture book *And Tango Makes Three* is inspired by a true story of inseparable male penguins, Roy and Silo. The two penguins caused a sensation at the Central Park Zoo in New York City when they tended an egg until it hatched and nurtured the chick together. When the book appeared in 2005, reviewers called it a heartwarming tale. Coauthors and real-life partners Peter Parnell and Justin Richardson intended it as a jumping-off point for parents to talk to their children about same-sex partnerships. Yet across the country, it was challenged, banned, or placed on restricted shelves in schools and public libraries. It held a spot on the ALA's annual most challenged books list for over a decade.

Conservative parent groups have claimed, incorrectly, that it is sexually explicit. The authors argue that these parents confuse sexuality with sex, which would never happen if the penguins were a male-female pair. The young readers for whom it was intended, however, love the book. When the authors were invited to schools to read the book, students cheered in delight when the egg hatches and the penguin chick, Tango, emerges. "Children see it as a story about family and trying to get something you want and finally getting it," Richardson says.

Quoted in Leonard S. Marcus, ed., *You Can't Say That: Writers for Young People Talk About Censorship, Free Expression, and the Stories They Have to Tell.* Somerville: MA: Candlewick, 2021, p. 158.

harshest words at public schools and libraries, which they blame for indoctrinating young people with LGBTQ books and curricula and pressuring them to conform to the new norms.

What Does It Mean to Be Age Appropriate?

Like the group behind the censorship of library Pride displays, parents who challenge books with LGBTQ themes believe they are shielding children from content that is inappropriate for them. They argue that when children are exposed to books that normalize LGBTQ characters and stories, they will be influenced to become gay (an idea that has been completely debunked.)

Many of the books under attack are YA titles in genres from fantasy to romance, memoir to realistic fiction. The target audience for YA is twelve- to eighteen-year-old readers, but because the developmental gap between a twelve- and an eighteen-year-old is wide, some books are marketed as "upper YA" and intended for older teens only. Most people agree that young children should not have access to books written for older, more mature readers, but there is little consensus about what it means to be age appropriate. Educators say a book is age appropriate for young people when they have the life experiences and cognitive skills to comprehend it.

In contrast, when many parent groups label a book as inappropriate, they usually mean that children should not be exposed to it because it has content that conflicts with their personal, religious, or political beliefs. In the case of children's or YA books with LGBTQ themes, civil rights groups point out that there is often a blatant double standard. Parents claim that the books are pornographic or obscene, but they rarely have the same objections to YA books that portray heterosexual relationships.

For decades, civil rights advocates say the rhetoric of protecting children from harm was used to justify discriminatory laws and practices against LGBTQ Americans that forced them to keep their sexual orientation hidden out of fear of harassment and violence. "[It's a] false flag—that parents are doing this to protect children," says author I.W. Gregorio. "Not a single child has ever been harmed by any of these books that have been banned. The only thing that has been harmed is perhaps parents' sensibilities."[26]

> "[It's a] false flag—that parents are doing this to protect children. Not a single child has ever been harmed by any of these books that have been banned. The only thing that has been harmed is perhaps parents' sensibilities."[26]
>
> —I.W. Gregorio, YA author

In the Classroom

As the moral panic over gender identity reached a fever pitch, many states began debating measures to ban classroom discussion about LGBTQ issues. In March 2022 Florida passed a bill

A teenager looks at books in the library. Many of the books under attack are young adult titles in genres ranging from fantasy to romance and from memoir to realistic fiction.

that has served as a model for other states, including Alabama and South Dakota.

Florida's new Parental Rights in Education Act prohibits public school teachers from holding any classroom instruction about sexual orientation or gender identity for students in kindergarten through third grade. In the fourth grade and up, the law bars any instruction on these issues if it is presented in a way that is not age appropriate. The law also allows parents to decide what is suitable for children and to sue schools they believe are in violation of the law. "Parents have every right to be informed about services offered to their child at school and should be protected from schools

> "Parents have every right to be informed about services offered to their child at school and should be protected from schools using classroom instruction to sexualize their kids as young as 5 years old."[27]
>
> —Florida governor Ron DeSantis

using classroom instruction to sexualize their kids as young as 5 years old,"[27] Florida governor Ron DeSantis declared after signing the bill into law.

Opponents of the law have dubbed it the "Don't Say Gay Law." Many teachers worry that it will stifle discussions out of fear and erase the lives and experiences of children with same-sex parents or relatives and of LGBTQ young people. Within weeks of its passage, LGBTQ rights groups, the American Civil Liberties Union, and others had filed lawsuits on behalf of Florida students and teachers to block the new law. They allege that it discriminates against LGBTQ students and educators and violates their civil rights.

The Most Challenged Book in America

When Maia Kobabe came out as gender nonbinary in 2016, there were few words to describe the experience. Kobabe's 2020 graphic memoir *Gender Queer* recounts that coming out story. The book contains a handful of drawings that are sexually explicit. After it won the ALA's Alex Award, for an adult book with special appeal to teens, many school librarians purchased it for their collections.

That award catapulted *Gender Queer* and its author into the spotlight. In the nine months of PEN America's 2021–2022 survey of book banning in US public schools, *Gender Queer* was challenged more than thirty times. Some lawmakers have claimed the right to remove the book from school libraries without a review process, because they say it is obscenity. Obscenity is one of the few categories of speech unprotected by the First Amendment. In fact, legal experts say, *Gender Queer* does not come close to meeting the court's narrow definition for obscenity.

Kobabe has been shaken by the negative attention. "Removing or restricting queer books in libraries and schools," the author says, "is like cutting a lifeline for queer youth who might not yet even know what terms to ask Google to find out more about their own identities, bodies and health."

Quoted in Victoria Rahbar, "*Gender Queer* Most Challenged of 2021," *Intellectual Freedom Blog*, Office for Intellectual Freedom of the American Library Association, April 4, 2022. www.oif.ala.org.

Children's Picture Books with LGBTQ Characters

In Florida, teaching about gender identity and sexuality is *not* part of the first-grade curriculum, but talking about families is. First-grade teachers have expressed concern that they will be in violation of the law if their students read and discuss picture books that show families with same-sex parents or children who do not conform to conventional gender ideas. Until recently, elementary-school-age children were unlikely to see any LGBTQ characters or stories portrayed in their picture books. In 1989 *Heather Has Two Mommies* broke new ground. Billed as a tale of love and acceptance about a little girl with two moms, it sparked fierce debate about LGBTQ content in children's literature. *Heather Has Two Mommies* appeared on the ALA's most challenged book list throughout the 1990s, and it is still often targeted by conservative parent groups.

Today there are more LGBTQ-themed, or rainbow, children's books than ever before. These include *Prince & Knight*, a spin on the classic fairy tale in which a prince weds a knight instead of a princess; *Julián Is a Mermaid*, which features a Latino boy who longs to be a dazzling mermaid; and *I Am Jazz*, the story of the author, Jazz Jennings, who transitioned from male to female at a young age. Sometimes LGBTQ issues are incidental to the plot, as in the picture book *Uncle Bobby's Wedding*, in which a girl celebrates her uncle's same-sex wedding. The story revolves around her worries that he will no longer have time to fly kites with her or take her to the ballet. In schools and libraries across the country, these books are frequently challenged and banned.

Young Adult Books with LGBTQ Themes

In recent years the publishing industry has also recognized a growing readership for YA books with LGBTQ characters and stories in all genres—from biographies of prominent LGBTQ figures to historical romances centered on gay and lesbian relationships. YA authors have shattered stereotypes—and broken taboos—by populating their books with gay, lesbian, transgender, or nonbinary vampires, denizens of fantasy worlds, and manga charac-

Book publishers have recognized a growing readership for YA books with LGBTQ characters and themes. Many of these books, including the coming-of-age memoir *All Boys Aren't Blue*, have provoked outrage among some parents and lawmakers.

ters. But the books that have provoked the most outrage are YA coming-of-age stories by LGBTQ authors that center on explorations of gender identity and sexuality. These titles often include emotionally raw, candid depictions of sexual encounters, bullying, mental health struggles, and sexual violence. While many upper YA books are more explicit than in the past, these titles are singled out. In 2021 the three books topping the ALA's most challenged of the year list included the graphic memoir *Gender Queer* by Maia Kobabe, which depicts the author's experiences of gender and sexuality while growing up and coming out as gender nonbinary; *All Boys Aren't Blue* by George M. Johnson, which chronicles the author's coming of age as a queer Black man; and *Lawn Boy* by

Jonathan Evison, which portrays a Mexican American young man wrestling with issues of race, class, and sexual identity. (*Gender Queer* and *Lawn Boy* are adult books, but the ALA has recognized both for their crossover appeal to older teens.)

Often backed by conservative advocacy groups, parents have crowded into school board meetings to rail against these books, demanding that their children's schools remove them from classrooms and libraries. Educators worry about the impact on an already vulnerable population when LGBTQ books are challenged and banned. According to 2020 Centers for Disease Control and Prevention (CDC) data, the roughly 11.2 percent of young people ages thirteen to seventeen who identify as LGBTQ were more likely than their peers to report anxiety, depression, and suicidal thoughts or to miss school due to safety concerns, such as bullying and harassment.

For many LGBTQ young people, especially those who do not have supportive home or school environments, books can be a lifeline. Many LGBTQ authors say they write the books they wish they could have turned to when they were struggling as teens. "There were no books for me to read in order to understand what I was going through as a kid," writes *All Boys Aren't Blue* author Johnson. "There were no heroes or icons to look up to and emulate. There were no road maps or guidelines for the journey. . . . Because I know there wasn't and still isn't much out there, I made it my original goal to get this right."[28]

CHAPTER FOUR

Banned and Challenged: Young Adult Novels That Push Boundaries

The news of the book ban in McMinn County, Tennessee, broke on January 26, 2021, the eve of Holocaust Remembrance Day. Every year on January 27, people around the world remember the 6 million Jews and millions of other people killed by the Nazis during World War II. The members of the local school board had removed the Pulitzer Prize–winning graphic nonfiction book *Maus* from their eighth-grade social studies curriculum. The vote was unanimous: 10–0 in favor of the ban.

Maus: A Survivor's Tale, originally published in 1986, is an eyewitness account of the Holocaust, based on author and cartoonist Art Spiegelman's interviews with his aging father, a Polish Jew and Holocaust survivor. In his stark black-and-white comic panels, Spiegelman depicts the Jewish victims as mice and their Nazi oppressors as cats: an allegory for the way the Nazis tried to dehumanize the Jews. The book portrays the unimaginable cruelties that Spiegelman's father witnessed, including forced labor and the gas chambers of the Auschwitz concentration camp. It also wrestles with the author's experiences as the child of Holocaust survivors, his stormy relationship with his father, and his mother's suicide. Educators say *Maus*'s comic book format makes it compelling and accessible in helping students engage with the horrific reality of the Holocaust.

At a special meeting to discuss the book's removal in McMinn County, a school board member asserted that he had no problem with students learning about the Holocaust. Rather, he added, it was the profanity, nudity, and depiction of suicide in *Maus* that made it inappropriate. A second board member remarked, "It shows people hanging. It shows them killing kids. Why does the education system promote this kind of stuff? It is not wise or healthy."[29] Across the country, many educators reacted with concern. They viewed the banning of *Maus* as part of a larger effort to erase books and curricula that shine a light on the oppression of minority religious, racial, and ethnic groups.

Grappling with Difficult Subject Matter

McMinn County teachers felt confident their eighth graders could handle the dark material in *Maus*. Even so when talking about *Maus* in the classroom, the teachers intended to guide the dis-

Comic Books and Graphic Novels Under the Microscope

Since Art Spiegelman's first volume of *Maus* appeared in 1986, many book-length comics have tackled serious subject matter. Yet according to the Comic Book Legal Defense Fund, comics and graphic novels are "uniquely susceptible to challenges and bans." They are visual, which makes it easy to take a single image out of context, and many people dismiss them as lowbrow and unserious.

The graphic novels that have come under the harshest attack in recent years include those with LGBTQ and racial themes, but comic book censorship has a long history in America. In 1954 child psychologist Fredric Wertham published a now infamous book called *Seduction of the Innocent*, in which he made false claims that reading comics led to juvenile delinquency. His work led to a public outcry. The US Senate held hearings that put comic books on trial. Rather than face government regulation, comic book publishers agreed to self-censor. For many decades, the Comics Code Authority (CCA) scrubbed comics clean of profanity, violence, sex, drugs, horror, vampires, werewolves, torture, and disrespect for authority figures. Since only comics with the CCA's seal could be sold in stores, publishers were forced to comply. Eventually, the comic book industry reinvented itself, and the CCA dissolved—but the taint remained.

Comic Book Legal Defense Fund, "Banned Comics," 2022. http://cbldf.org.

cussion and help students through any discomfort. Among authors and publishers, debate has long raged over what is too violent, sexually explicit, or disturbing to include in books that teen readers process on their own, without a teacher's guidance. As cultural attitudes about profanity, sexuality, drug use, and other social issues have shifted—and teens have gained access to a world of content online—many of the taboos that once applied to YA books have faded away.

The YA category emerged in the 1960s, but its popularity exploded in the early 2000s with the *Harry Potter* series and the vampire-themed romance *The Twilight Saga*. In realistic, contemporary upper YA novels, characters swear, use sexual slang and innuendo, become physically intimate, drink and use drugs, and cope with mental health issues or sexual abuse. They also rebel against the adults in their lives and sometimes inflict harm on themselves or others. Yet publishers and authors walk a tight-rope: YA books cannot be too explicit or they will be marketed for adults. Publishers say that what makes these books YA as opposed to adult is their focus on teen protagonists, and their voice, which must ring true to teen readers.

Although some adults view the content of the new, edgy YA as too disturbing or inappropriate, authors counter that many young people experience painful situations in childhood—or they may know someone who has. They say that books are one of the safest places for teens to confront difficult subject matter. "The characters in teen novels push boundaries and face daunting obstacles as they evolve into the people they want to become," explains award-winning author Elizabeth Acevedo. "They often make risky, hair-raising choices and face unexpected consequences. This . . . reflects the messy and often heartbreaking process of growing up."[30]

> "The characters in teen novels push boundaries and face daunting obstacles as they evolve into the people they want to become. They often make risky, hair-raising choices and face unexpected consequences. This . . . reflects the messy and often heartbreaking process of growing up."[30]
>
> —Elizabeth Acevedo, YA author

YA Authors Who Paved the Way

In the earliest years of YA literature, books that addressed social issues often took the form of problem novels. Literary critics explain that these were written to dissuade readers from following in the path of the main characters, who faced problems such as teen pregnancy and drug addiction. When it was published in 1971, *Go Ask Alice* was billed as the real diary of a fifteen-year-old girl that was found after her drug overdose death. Its entries are filled with profanity, descriptions of drug parties, prostitution, and sexual abuse. It was later revealed that the diary was a fake, and today many readers find it unrealistic rather than shocking. Yet for years *Go Ask Alice* was challenged for its scandalous content. It was one of the books removed from a high school library that sparked the Supreme Court's landmark *Pico* book-banning case.

In the decades after *Go Ask Alice*, YA books that explored serious social issues still often warned against the dangers of risky behaviors, but the characters were less one-dimensional and the stories less moralistic. Popular YA author John Green has been candid about his own struggles with obsessive-compulsive disorder and anxiety—and his characters often cope with similar issues. His most challenged title, *Looking for Alaska*, is set in a boarding school in Alabama. The teen characters swear, use drugs, smoke cigarettes, and have sex—and there is a fatal accident that may or not be suicide.

YA author John Green says parents too often read explicit passages out of context. These passages only reflect part of the multilayered characters that populate his books.

Yet Green complains that parents read the explicit passages out of context, and he defends his decision to include them.

Among the pioneers who paved the way for today's realistic YA novels, Judy Blume influenced a generation with her relatable teen girl characters. Her books were among the first to openly explore puberty, teen sexuality, and body image. In her 1970 title *Are You There, God? It's Me Margaret*, an almost twelve-year-old Margaret prays to God to get her period, wrestles with sanitary products, and starts to feel attracted to boys. As one of the most challenged authors of the twenty-first century, Blume has become a fierce advocate for the right to read. "Even if you removed all objectionable (to censors) books from the schools and libraries," she says, "you can't stop children from thinking about things written about in those books."[31]

Edgy YA Content

They are set in other worlds and include characters with supernatural powers, but YA fantasy, science-fiction, horror, and dystopian novels still reflect the concerns of contemporary teen readers. In recent years the titles in these genres that are most likely to be challenged also feature LGBTQ or racially diverse characters.

Echo Brown and Tiffany D. Jackson are YA authors whose novels grapple with issues such as sexism, racism, sexual abuse, depression, and drug addiction. Yet their books are also often infused with magic or horror and the supernatural. In the semiautobiographical, *Black Girl Unlimited*, Brown portrays a young Black girl wizard who travels between the despair of her poor urban neighborhood and a wealthy school across the city. With her powers, she can see the black veils of pain that descend on and suffocate many people in her community. Jackson's *White Smoke* profiles a Black teen girl who struggles with anxiety and substance abuse. The riveting plot unfolds as she moves with her interracial family to a haunted house.

Both authors' books have been challenged and banned from school libraries. "I'm realizing it's not about the book at all," Jackson says, "it's about the children the book is highlighting and the color of their skin."

Quoted in Elliott C. McLaughlin, "Book Banning in the US: These Are the Authors of Color Who Censors Are Trying to Silence," CNN, June 4, 2022. www.cnn.com.

Drug and Alcohol Use

Parents have often objected to YA books that depict drug and alcohol use, claiming that they glamorize illegal drugs and tempt teens to try them. Even early YA problem novels that carried strong antidrug messages were often challenged. In recent years adult marijuana use has become legal in many places, and a devastating opioid crisis has claimed tens of thousands of lives across the country. Rather than try to shock or scare readers, some YA books offer sympathetic portrayals of people whose lives and families have been upended by addiction.

In 2018 Jarrett J. Krosoczka, whose *Lunch Lady* series is a laugh-out-loud favorite with younger readers, turned to a serious and deeply personal topic. His graphic YA memoir, *Hey, Kiddo*, depicts his teen years. During these years, Krosoczka lived with his grandparents, who drank heavily and verbally abused him. He also exchanged letters with his absent, heroin-addicted mother. *Hey, Kiddo* has been challenged by parents for vulgar language and inappropriate behavior. "If my student walked into the principal's office and called any teacher one of these names they'd be disciplined immediately. So why is it okay for them to read it?"[32] asked one Iowa parent who filed a complaint against the book.

> "If my student walked into the principal's office and called any teacher one of these names they'd be disciplined immediately. So why is it okay for them to read it?"[32]
>
> —An Iowa parent who challenged *Hey, Kiddo*

Krosoczka defends his decision not to filter out the gritty content. "My grandparents chain-smoked, drank heavily, and cursed constantly," he explains. "And that was the part of my childhood that was a refuge from the darker more dangerous life that my mother led. It would have been disingenuous and a disservice to readers if I sanitized the story."[33]

Mental Health Issues

For several years YA books in which characters struggled with mental health issues and trauma often focused on teen suicide. The trend began with Jay Asher's 2007 best-selling book

Thirteen Reasons Why. From the start, the book raised red flags with mental health counselors and parents for romanticizing suicide. The book first earned a spot on the ALA's most challenged list in 2012. It would later top the list after the book was adapted into a popular TV series in 2017.

The novel and TV series follow a high school boy who receives a box of thirteen cassette tapes, prerecorded by a classmate who died by suicide. On the tapes, she describes her reasons for killing herself and calls out the people she holds responsible. To many critics, her voice on the tapes, speaking from beyond the grave, softens the finality of suicide. Rather than a young life cut tragically short, it feels like a teen girl's revenge story. In 2020 the CDC reported that suicide was the second-leading cause of death for young people ages ten to twenty-four. Many mental health counselors worried that the book would discourage teens who suffered from depression or trauma from seeking help.

Recent YA books continue to address suicide and also offer unflinching portraits of teens grappling with mental health issues such as self-harm and depression. But as author Adib Khorram explains, "Lately, there have been books that look at mental illness as a part of a person rather than a crisis."[34] Authors like Khorram hope these portrayals will break the stigma of mental illness and help readers realize that their mental health struggles do not have to define them. Increasingly, these books also include racially diverse and LGBTQ characters. In Khorram's *Darius the Great Is Not Okay*, fifteen-year-old Darius suffers from depression and low self-esteem, but that is only one part of his identity. He is also an avid tea drinker and *Star Trek* fan who is questioning his sexuality and exploring his cultural heritage as a biracial, half-Iranian teen. Khorram's book was banned in several Texas schools in 2021. As a Muslim and queer teen who suffered from depression, Khorram felt erased from the books he read growing up. He worries that book banning will have the same effect on the young people he writes for today.

Sexual Harassment and Sexual Violence

In 1999 author Laurie Halse Anderson shattered one of the last taboos in YA literature: talking about sexual violence. In her acclaimed novel *Speak*, the protagonist is raped by a senior while drunk at a summer party before her freshman year of high school. Traumatized by the rape, and bullied by classmates, she is unable to speak, except to utter what is absolutely necessary. Although the book contains no explicit content, it is often challenged by conservative parent groups, which have called it pornographic and biased against male students. Defenders counter that the book helps students understand what survivors of traumatic experiences endure and how peers and teachers can recognize the signs and support them.

Anderson opened the door for other YA authors to address sexual harassment and sexual violence in their books. Author Elizabeth Acevedo is a sharp critic of sexism and so-called rape

The Poet X *by Elizabeth Acevedo was removed from library shelves in one Virginia school and challenged by parents at another school. The author is pictured here at a 2018 book signing.*

culture—a conceptual environment that includes the idea that victims bring sexual violence on themselves by dressing or acting a certain way or by not taking the right precautions. Her 2018 award-winning YA novel, *The Poet X*, features a fifteen-year-old Afro-Latina protagonist who has a full, curvy figure and struggles with unwanted attention and harassment from the young men in her Harlem, New York, neighborhood. She also fights with her devout, churchgoing mother who body-shames her for her figure. Eventually, she learns to accept her body and, like Acevedo herself, to find her voice in spoken-word poetry. In 2021 a Virginia school pulled *The Poet X* from library shelves after a parent complained about the character's sexualization. Another Virginia family filed a lawsuit against their child's school for teaching the book, contending that it disparaged their Christian faith. (The judge ruled in favor of the school district.)

In response to these and other incidents, YA author Meg Medina pleaded with officials in her home state of Virginia and across the country to put a stop to book bans. "To pull books from a school library because of the discomfort they create in adults is a recipe for disaster," she wrote. "It supports a false idea that there is one version of life that is acceptable. And, it denigrates the work of authors who are brave enough to name experiences that are difficult and real."[35]

CHAPTER FIVE

Teaching and Learning: Caught Between Polarized Views

Acclaimed author and poet Nikki Grimes has been writing books for more than four decades. Yet in March 2022 she was surprised to hear from a teacher that school officials had blocked him from using her YA novel *Bronx Masquerade* in his eighth-grade social studies classroom. The teacher, who asked to remain anonymous, told Grimes that he knew his school did not have the funds to purchase the book, so he raised the money himself and bought two hundred copies for his students.

Bronx Masquerade tells the story of a fictional English class in an inner-city New York high school where the teen characters share their lives and vulnerabilities through open-mic poetry. The teacher who contacted Grimes believed his eighth graders would relate to the story, since they were dealing with many of the same issues in their own lives as the characters in Grimes's novel. But when he approached school officials, they refused to allow him to teach the book. They objected to its mild profanity and references to racism, drugs, sex, and teen pregnancy.

Grimes warns that authors and educators must be vigilant about these quiet incidents of book banning. In May 2022 she was one of thirteen hundred children's and YA authors who signed a letter sponsored by the group We Need Diverse

Books condemning efforts to purge diverse books from the nation's schools. The letter appealed to Congress, state legislatures, and school boards to address the problem. Grimes's award-winning 2019 memoir in verse, *Ordinary Hazards*, has also been challenged and removed from school libraries. It chronicles her harrowing childhood, growing up in poverty with a mother who suffered from paranoid schizophrenia and alcoholism and a father who was periodically absent from her life. Throughout her turbulent childhood, Grimes was saved by books and writing. "Not every young adult is privileged to have a home library," she says. "Those readers rely entirely upon school and public libraries for their access to books, as I did, growing up. Without such access, I've no idea what would have become of me. I shudder to think."[36]

The Social Studies Wars

Far from the big-city school that Grimes depicts in *Bronx Masquerade*, in a classroom in rural Washington County, Oklahoma, brand-new copies of another book, *Killers of the Flower Moon*, were stacked up unread. High school teacher Debra Thoreson had ordered the books for her eleventh-grade students, but after Oklahoma's divisive concepts law, HB 1775, took effect in July 2021, she decided she could not risk assigning it. Like dozens of such laws passed in recent years, HB 1775 bans the teaching of any lesson that causes students to feel discomfort or guilt because of their race or sex. It also gives parents the right to file a complaint with the school district if they dislike what their children are learning. Thoreson worried that her teacher's license could be suspended if she were found to be in violation of the law.

Killers of the Flower Moon is an award-winning nonfiction book, in which journalist David Grann re-

"Not every young adult is privileged to have a home library. Those readers rely entirely upon school and public libraries for their access to books, as I did, growing up. Without such access, I've no idea what would have become of me."[36]

—Nikki Grimes, children's and YA author and poet

Some Oklahoma teachers fear teaching *Killers of the Flower Moon* because of the state's new divisive concepts law. The book recounts real events involving racist federal policies, land theft, and murder perpetrated against members of Oklahoma's Osage Nation.

counts a little-known, devastating episode in US history. After oil was discovered under Osage Nation land in Oklahoma in the early 1900s, tribal members briefly became some of the richest people in the world. And then many of them were brutally murdered and their oil rights stolen. The book addresses racist US government policies, Native American land theft, murder, and cultural damage. It is dark, unsettling history, but it is also tightly interwoven with the history of Oklahoma, which has the second-largest Native American population of any state in the country (after Alaska).

Restrictive laws like HB 1775 are new and extreme measures, but scholars say that teaching about the country's history has always been political. In fact, controversies over what gets written into American history textbooks are so common that they have a name: "the social studies wars." Many educators stress that thinking critically about the past helps students better understand the present. But to some conservative groups, focusing on stories of injustice and oppression, rather than on the great figures of US history or American exceptionalism—the idea that

49

No Longer Safe Spaces for Students?

By law, parents or guardians have always been able to access their children's school library records or request that they be restricted from checking out certain books. But many librarians say new tracking measures are harmful to students. Software programs notify parents when their children check out books and allow parents to monitor children's library records online.

Such measures may place vulnerable students at greater risk. According to the LGBTQ-advocacy group Human Rights Campaign, only 25 percent of LGBTQ youth are able to be out at home. Notifying parents that students are exploring their sexuality or reading LGBTQ-themed books could lead to emotional or physical abuse. The greatest danger, says Book Riot editor Danika Ellis, "is to queer kids and teens whose parents are unsupportive, students looking for safer sex information, children with abusive parents looking for resources to keep themselves safe, and more. For these students the library could be the safest place they can go."

Danika Ellis, "Technology for Parent Monitoring of Student Library Use Is Being Developed by Follett: This Week's Book Censorship News," Book Riot, April 1, 2022. https://bookriot.com.

the country's values, history, and political system are unique in the world—is unpatriotic.

The tribal nations in Oklahoma have incredible stories to tell, says former Osage Nation chief principal Jim Gray, but under HB 1775, students are unlikely to hear them. When he noticed a photo of the stacked-up copies of *Killers of the Flower Moon* posted on social media, he was troubled. "We don't study history to feel good about it," he says. "History is there for us to understand the mistakes of the past so we cannot repeat them."[37]

Rethinking the Classics

For generations, American literature curricula across the country have included books from the high school canon. These are titles that many people believe should be read by everyone who attends high school in the United States. They include *The Scarlet Letter*, *To Kill a Mockingbird*, *Huckleberry Finn*, and *The Great Gatsby*. While some of these books continue to exert a strong influence on the culture, they do not reflect the diversity of experiences in America.

Two of the most controversial works in the high school canon are also among the most beloved: *To Kill a Mockingbird* by Harper Lee (1960) and *Huckleberry Finn* by Mark Twain (1885). In 2021 several school districts made headlines when they removed these books from the curriculum. They said the books were removed because they contain racist language, including the N-word, and promote White savior narratives—in which a heroic, central White character rescues a secondary Black character. Black parents insisted that their children should not have to endure being made to feel uncomfortable during class discussions of the books.

In many schools, *Huckleberry Finn* and *To Kill a Mockingbird* are the two main literary works used to examine racial oppression and the history of Jim Crow laws (state and local statutes

To Kill a Mockingbird has long been used in schools to teach about racial oppression and Jim Crow laws. In 2021 several school districts removed this book from the curriculum after some Black parents expressed concerns about how the characters are depicted.

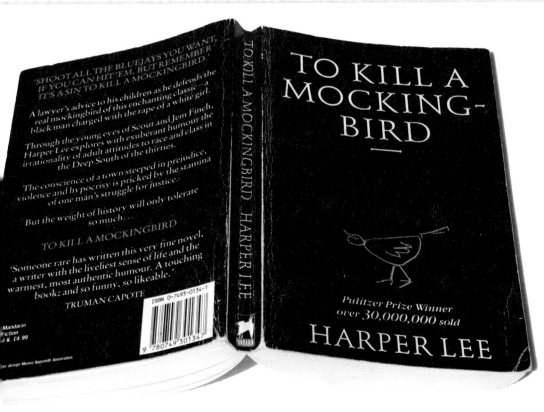

that legalized racial segregation) in the American South. Yet their Black characters are stuttering, one-dimensional figures. In 2017 author and activist Alice Randall struck a chord with some educators—and provoked social media outrage among *To Kill a Mockingbird*'s die-hard fans. In an online editorial for NBC News, she wrote, "The book cannot continue to be taught as if every person in the classroom is white, upper middle class and needs to be prodded into being Scout [the novel's young protagonist, who is slowly awakened to racial injustice]. . . . Imagine instead that you are an African-American eighth-grade boy in Mississippi today, and are asked to read 'Mockingbird.'"[38]

The free speech group National Coalition Against Censorship rejects this view and has fought against efforts to remove *To Kill a Mockingbird* and *Huckleberry Finn* from the curriculum. The group argues that these iconic texts shaped American culture

The Toll on Teachers and Librarians

In 2022 in Llano County, Texas, a school librarian was fired after she refused to follow instructions to purge the library of books deemed objectionable. In New Hampshire a local chapter of Moms for Liberty offered to pay a $500 bounty to any parent who turned in a teacher for violating the state's restrictive new divisive concepts law. In Annandale, New Jersey, a veteran school librarian was shocked when a parent at a school board meeting publicly accused her of being a pornographer.

Teachers and librarians are on the front lines of America's culture war. They have been slandered on social media by people who claim they are giving children access to pornographic and obscene books. In some states they fear losing their jobs or costing their schools much-needed state funding if they do not censor their teaching. Some politicians have even proposed measures to treat librarians as criminals for disseminating materials the politicians label as harmful to minors. "It's crushing," says retired Texas librarian Carolyn Foote. "You know what your job is, you know what the best practices and standards are for your profession, and you're being made to do things that you know violate all that."

Quoted in Elizabeth A. Harris and Alexandra Alter, "With Rising Book Bans, Librarians Have Come Under Attack," *New York Times*, July 6, 2022. www.nytimes.com.

and help students understand the historical realities of racism. Some educators have proposed a middle ground, in which students read the two novels alongside literary works by prominent Black authors that include more fully realized Black characters.

The Battle over Sex Education

Beyond academic subjects like literature and history, some of the fiercest culture war battles are waged over sex education. America has long been conflicted over how to promote sexual health to young people. The country's media, movies, and video games are awash in sexualized images, yet some groups fight any efforts to provide students with accurate information about sex and the human body. As of 2020, according to the nonprofit group Sex Ed for Social Change, twenty-nine states plus Washington, DC, mandated sex education in schools. In the other twenty-one states, sexual health curricula were haphazard. Some offered a week of instruction; others, none at all. In six states, laws require that sexual health instruction describe LGBTQ relationships as unacceptable or prohibit mentioning them at all.

For decades, groups such as the Family Policy Alliance, Focus on the Family, and, more recently, Moms for Liberty have pushed to restrict students' access to medically accurate information about topics such as pregnancy, contraception, and sexuality. They have also successfully lobbied for many school districts to adopt abstinence-only before marriage approaches to sex education. With the latest culture war, civil rights groups warn, their tactics have become more extreme as they mobilize to block schools from including the experiences of LGBTQ students.

These groups often target their attacks at a curriculum called Comprehensive Sex Education (CSE). First developed in the 1990s by Sex Ed for Social Change and adopted by a growing number of school districts, CSE teaches students about much more than basic anatomy. The curriculum also covers bodily changes during puberty, how to prevent pregnancy and sexually transmitted diseases, consent and healthy relationships, contraception, gender identity, and sexual orientation. It also presents information on abortion. The groups opposed to its teaching frame it as a parents' rights issue. "While I'm raising my children with biblically based morals and values at home," writes Stephanie Curry of the Family Policy Alliance, "schools are undermining and refuting those same lessons in the classroom."[39]

The Family Policy Alliance and other groups have been accused of spreading fear and misinformation online. They have pushed to ban books that address sexual health in school libraries, disrupted school board meetings, injected anti-LGTBQ rhetoric into political campaigns, and sometimes publicly released the names of transgender students to open them up to bullying and harassment.

School Libraries Under Siege

For LGBTQ students and others who may be vulnerable to bullying, school libraries—now often called media centers—have long served as safe, welcoming spaces. They are staffed by librarians who create collections that appeal to a diversity of students and encourage lifelong reading. In the Supreme Court's 1982 *Pico* decision, Justice William J. Brennan Jr. recognized the school library as a place where "the selection of books is entirely a matter of free choice" and students have "an opportunity at self-education and individual enrichment."[40]

Yet that vision is increasingly out of touch with reality, as free speech groups warn that school libraries have become the targets of efforts to curtail students' intellectual freedom. Some state legislatures and departments of education have begun to use the power of government to crack down on school libraries. They are restricting the books librarians are permitted to order, subjecting any new books to a public review, and making it easier for parents to keep tabs on the books and materials their children check out.

Even without mandates from the state, local school districts have also tightened the reins on school libraries. In some districts, parents get an email notification every time their child checks out a book. Most educators hope that parents will guide their children's reading and talk to them about the ideas in books in relation to their own values. However, they argue that the new measures threaten students' ability to read and think in an environment free from surveillance.

Students Push Back Against Book Banning

If there is any silver lining in the latest wave of book banning, free speech advocates point to the groundswell of student activism it has provoked. Across the country, thousands of middle and high school students are pushing back against the bans. They have organized public protests and spoken out at school

Idaho students protest the decision by the Nampa School District board to remove books from the district's libraries. As part of their 2022 protest, the students are reading some of the banned books.

board meetings and statehouses. Some have sought donations of banned books and distributed them to fellow students. Others have formed book clubs to read and discuss the titles that some adults in the community have deemed too dangerous, too uncomfortable, or inappropriate for them.

Christina Ellis is one of those student activists. In November 2020 her Pennsylvania school district voted to put a freeze on hundreds of books and other materials that appeared on a list compiled by a school diversity committee. The list had been intended as a resource guide for students and teachers who were grappling with the turmoil that followed the police killing of George Floyd. It included *Hidden Figures*, a biography of the Black women scientists who worked on the early US space program; *Malala: My Story of Standing Up for Girls' Rights*, by the young Pakistani human rights activist and Nobel Peace Prize winner; and Ibram X. Kendi's *How to Be an Anti-Racist*. A group of parents objected to the books on the grounds that they would be used to indoctrinate students and make White children feel uncomfortable and guilty about their race.

> "We are better with education. We are better with knowledge."[41]
>
> —Christina Ellis, Central York Pennsylvania High School student activist

Ellis and her fellow student activists staged peaceful protests outside their high school every morning at 7:15 a.m. before the bell rang. They attended school board meetings, wrote letters to the local newspaper, read from the banned books on Instagram, and spoke to national media. Under intense pressure, the school board finally reversed its decision and lifted the freeze. "As a Black student who sits in these classes it's also uncomfortable for me," Ellis told reporters. "We are better with education. We are better with knowledge."[41]

SOURCE NOTES

Introduction:
A New Wave of Book Banning

1. Matt Krause, "Letter to Texas Education Agency and School Superintendents," Texas Tribune, October 25, 2021. www.texastribune.org.
2. Quoted in Corky Siemaszko, "Texas Lawmaker Says 850 Books Ranging from Race to Sexuality Could Cause 'Discomfort,'" NBC News, October 27, 2021. www.nbcnews.com.
3. Quoted in Siemaszko, "Texas Lawmaker Says 850 Books Ranging from Race to Sexuality Could Cause 'Discomfort.'"
4. Quoted in Rafael Medoff, "Helen Keller vs. the Nazis," David S. Wyman Institute for Holocaust Studies, 2013. http://new.wymaninstitute.org.

Chapter One:
Book Bans, Culture Wars, and the Freedom to Read

5. Quoted in Elizabeth Blair, "During Banned Books Week, Readers Explore What It Means to Challenge Texts," NPR, September 30, 2021. www.npr.org.
6. Jonathan Friedman et al., "Banned in the USA: Rising School Book Bans Threaten Free Expression and Students' First Amendment Rights," PEN America, 2022. https://pen.org.
7. Quoted in PEN America, "Missing from the Shelf: Book Challenges and Lack of Diversity in Children's Literature," August 31, 2016. https://pen.org.
8. Quoted in No Left Turn in Education, "Battle on the Bookshelf: NLTE Is Exposing the Sexually Explicit and Predatory Content in Children's Books!," *Reporting from the Battlefield* newsletter, February 24, 2022. www.noleftturn.us.
9. Emma Sarappo, "This Is a Shakedown: Texas Has a Book-Banning Problem," *The Atlantic*, December 8, 2021. www.theatlantic.com.
10. Daniel José Older, "The Real Censorship in Children's Books: Smiling Slaves Is Just the Half of It," *The Guardian* (Manchester, UK), January 29, 2016. www.theguardian.com.
11. Suzanne Nossel, *Dare to Speak: Defending Free Speech for All.* New York: Dey St., 2020, p. 38.
12. Quoted in Valerie Nye and Kathy Barco, eds., *True Stories of Censorship Battles in America's Libraries.* Chicago: American Library Association Editions, 2012, p. 20.
13. *Board of Education, Island Trees Union Free School District No. 26 v. Pico*, 457 US 853, 1982.
14. Quoted in April Dawkins, "The *Pico* Case—35 Years Later," *Intellectual Freedom Blog*, Office for Intellectual Freedom of the American Library Association, November 7, 2017. www.oif.ala.org.

Chapter Two:
Banned and Challenged: Books That Address Race

15. Quoted in *Laura Murphy—McAuliffe Shut Us Out*, Youngkin Campaign for Virginia Governor, October 25, 2021. www.youtube.com/watch?v=LDB 4eLc5rfo.

16. Quoted in Kiara Alfonseca, "Critical Race Theory in the Classroom: Understanding the Debate," ABC News, May 19, 2021. https://abcnews.go .com.

17. Quoted in Kelly Jensen, "New Report Showcases Wide Damage of Educational Gag Orders," Book Riot, November 9, 2021. https://bookriot.com.

18. Quoted in Katie LaGrone, "Founders of Controversial Moms for Liberty Group Set Record Straight on Who They Are and Who They're Not," ABC Action News, December 3, 2021. www.abcactionnews.com.

19. Quoted in Valerie Strauss, "Imagine a Class with 25 Kids—and All of Their Parents Insist on Telling the Teacher What to Teach," *Washington Post*, October 28, 2021. www.washingtonpost.com.

20. Quoted in Mary Louise Kelly et al., "Ruby Bridges on Turning Her Experience of Desegregating a School into a Kids' Book," *All Things Considered*, NPR, September 5, 2022. www.npr.org.

21. Quoted in Andrew Stanton, "Tennessee Education Dept. Rejects Complaint That MLK Book Is 'Anti-White Teaching,'" *Newsweek*, November 29, 2021. www.newsweek.com.

22. Quoted in David K. Li, "Texas School District Pulls Books by Acclaimed Black Author Amid Critical Race Theory Claims," NBC News, October 6, 2021. www.nbc.com.

Chapter Three:
Banned and Challenged: Books with LGBTQ Themes

23. "CatholicVote Launches 'Hide the Pride' to Empty Libraries of LGBTQ Content Aimed at Kids," CatholicVote, June 3, 2022. www.catholicvote.org.

24. Deborah Caldwell-Stone, "Fight Censorship: Keeping PRIDE Books on Display," *Intellectual Freedom Blog*, Office for Intellectual Freedom of the American Library Association, June 9, 2022. www.oif.ala.org.

25. Kim Parker et al., "Americans' Complex Views on Gender Identity and Transgender Issues," Pew Research Center, June 28, 2022. www.pew research.org.

26. Quoted in EveryLibrary, "Censored Authors Speak: A Roundtable Discussion of Book Banning in America," April 6, 2022. www.everylibrary.org.

27. Quoted in Governor Ron DeSantis (website), "Governor Ron DeSantis Signs Historic Bill to Protect Parental Rights in Education," March 28, 2022. https://flgov.com.

28. George M. Johnson, *All Boys Aren't Blue*. New York: Farrar, Straus, and Giroux, 2020, p. 295.

Chapter Four:
Banned and Challenged: Young Adult Novels That Push Boundaries

29. Quoted in Dan Mangan, "Tennessee School Board Bans Holocaust Graphic Novel 'Maus'—Author Art Spiegelman Condemns the Move as 'Orwellian,'" CNBC, January 26, 2022. www.cnbc.com.

30. Quoted in Rebecca Slocum, "Happy Birthday Elizabeth Acevedo!," *Intellectual Freedom Blog*, Office for Intellectual Freedom of the American Library Association, February 15, 2022. www.oif.ala.org.

31. Quoted in Barbara Karlin, "Blume Speaks Out on Speaking Out," *Los Angeles Times*, October 18, 1981. www.latimes.com.

32. Quoted in Scott Carpenter, "Parent Files Formal Complaint About 'Vulgar' Book at Urbandale School," KCCI Des Moines, November 10, 2021. www.kcci.com.

33. Quoted in Steve Pfarrer, "Censorship Is Not the Answer: Children's Author and Illustrator Jarrett Krosoczka Says He's Deeply Troubled by Attempts to Ban Books from School Libraries," *Daily Hampshire Gazette* (Northampton, MA), December 10, 2021. www.gazettenet.com.

34. Quoted in Jessica Mizzi, "Adib Khorram on Writing Honestly About Mental Health, Love, and Iran," Brightly (Penguin Random House), 2022. www.readbrightly.com.

35. Meg Medina, "Stop the Madness: Banning Books Is Not the Answer," Meg Medina (website), October 30, 2021. https://megmedina.com.

Chapter Five:
Teaching and Learning: Caught Between Polarized Views

36. Nikki Grimes, "Banned Books: Message Rewind," *Nikki Sounds Off: An Occasional Blog*, March 21, 2022. www.nikkigrimes.com.

37. Quoted in Cassidy Mudd, "Tribal Leader Concerned HB 1775 Affecting How Native History Is Taught in Classroom," Public Radio Tulsa, August 14, 2022. www.publicradiotulsa.org.

38. Alice Randall, "Why Are We Still Teaching 'To Kill a Mockingbird' in Schools?," NBC News, October 19, 2017. www.nbcnews.com.

39. Stephanie Curry, "How to Stop Schools from Parenting Your Children," Daily Signal, December 18, 2020. www.dailysignal.com.

40. *Board of Education, Island Trees Union Free School District No. 26 v. Pico*, 457 US 853, 1982.

41. Quoted in Michel Martin, "2 Students Who Helped Reverse Their High School's Book Ban," *All Things Considered*, NPR, November 7, 2021. www.npr.org.

ORGANIZATIONS AND WEBSITES

American Library Association (ALA)

www.ala.org

The ALA supports public and school libraries and librarians across the country and defends against censorship. Its website provides a link to the Unite Against Book Bans campaign, resources to fight censorship in every US state and territory, its annual Most Challenged Books lists, and a form to report book-banning incidents in local school and public libraries.

Banned Books Week

www.bannedbooksweek.org

Every September, the ALA and a coalition of free speech and human rights groups host Banned Books Week to celebrate the right to read. The site features news, events, ways to get involved, printable flyers and posters, and a link to a Virtual Readout YouTube channel in which authors and their fans read excerpts from favorite banned books.

Cato Institute

www.cato.org

This libertarian public policy research organization believes that government should have a limited role in US society and individuals should be free to act as they choose so long as they do not hurt others. The site links to articles and blog posts by Cato scholars and offers a libertarian perspective on issues such as censorship, critical race theory, the 1619 Project, and book banning in schools.

Comic Book Legal Defense Fund

http://cbldf.org

The Comic Book Legal Defense works to protect the First Amendment rights of comic book and graphic novel creators, publishers, and readers by providing information and legal support. Its "Resources" page includes articles on the history of comic book censorship, printable "Know Your Rights" posters, and lists of comics, manga, and graphic novels that have recently been challenged or banned.

Fandom Forward

fandomforward.org

Fandom Forward works to turn fans of diverse books, comics, and manga into joyful activists. Its Book Defenders campaign promotes actions such as speaking out against book bans, creating art that celebrates a banned book, sending emails to support teen activists in other communities, and donating used books to a community in need.

The Foundation for Individual Rights and Expression (FIRE)
www.thefire.org
Directed by libertarian author and activist Greg Lukianoff, FIRE advocates for free speech rights on college campuses and in K–12 schools. Its members fight against what they view as political correctness and indoctrination by left-leaning educators in the classroom. The site links to articles and resources related to K–12 free speech rights and an essay contest open to US high school students.

GLSEN
www.glsen.org
GLSEN creates supportive, affirming environments for LGBTQ young people in K–12 schools. The News and Stories section links to a blog, articles, reviews of "rainbow books," and first-person stories told by students and LGBTQ community members. There are also tips for forming a Gay-Straight Alliance and donating LGBTQ-themed books to students.

National Coalition Against Censorship (NCAC)
https://ncac.org
For fifty years the NCAC has acted as a "first responder" to protect Americans' freedom of expression. Its Kids' Right to Read Project and Defend LGBTQ Stories campaign offer practical resources, including a handbook to support students facing book bans with background on First Amendment rights, advocacy tips, letter-writing templates, and sample social media posts.

PEN America
https://pen.org
Founded by a group of prominent US authors in the 1920s, PEN America unites authors, journalists, other writers, and their allies across the country and around the world to defend freedom of expression. PEN's reports *Educational Gag Orders* and *Banned in the USA* provide useful overviews of the censorship landscape across the country. Other resources include student tip sheets for fighting book bans, an index of book challenges, and a list of bans by state.

We Need Diverse Books
https://diversebooks.org
We Need Diverse Books is a group of children's book lovers and authors that advocates for changes in the publishing industry and promotes books that honor and reflect the lives of diverse young people. Resources include links to sites that review diverse children's and YA titles, as well as an Our Story app to help readers discover diverse books.

FOR FURTHER RESEARCH

Books

Victoria Heyworth Dunne, ed., *Banned Books: The World's Most Controversial Books, Past and Present*. New York: DK, 2022.

Marcia Amidon Lusted, ed., *Banned Books*. New York: Greenhaven, 2018.

Leonard S. Marcus, ed., *You Can't Say That! Writers for Young People Talk About Censorship, Free Expression, and the Stories They Have to Tell*. Somerville, MA: Candlewick, 2021.

Suzanne Nossel, *Dare to Speak: Defending Free Speech for All*. New York: Dey Street, 2020.

Internet Sources

Danika Ellis, "All 850 Books Texas Lawmaker Matt Krause Wants to Ban: An Analysis," Book Riot, November 5, 2021. https://bookriot.com.

Dana Goldstein, "Two States. Eight Textbooks. Two American Stories: American History Textbooks Can Differ Across the Country, in Ways That Are Shaded by Partisan Politics," *New York Times*, January 12, 2020. www.nytimes.com.

Erika Hayasaki et al., "Eye of the Storm: How Educators and Students Are Navigating the Hyperpoliticized Terrain of American Education," *New York Times Magazine*, September 11, 2022. www.nytimes.com.

Mike Hixenbaugh and Antonia Hylton, hosts, *Southlake Podcast: Inside a Critical Race Theory Battle*, NBC News, 2021. www.nbcnew.com.

Micah Loewinger, "Inside the SCOTUS Case on School Library Censorship," *On the Media*, WNYC Studios, February 4, 2022. www.wnycstudios.org.

Hannah Natanson and Lori Rozsa, "Students Lose Access to Books Amid 'State-Sponsored Purging of Ideas,'" *Washington Post*, August 17, 2022. www.washingtonpost.com.

Julia Rittenberg, "The History of Nazi Book Burning," Book Riot, April 6, 2022. https://bookriot.com.

Kate Shuster, *Teaching Hard History: American Slavery*. Montgomery, AL: Southern Poverty Law Center, 2018. www.splcenter.org.

Mark Walsh, "Yanking Books from School Libraries: What the Supreme Court Has Said, and Why It's Murky," Education Week, December 15, 2021. www.edweek.org.

INDEX